FriendZone

By

David Proud

This is a work of fiction. Names and characters are the product of the author's imagination and any resemblance to actual persons, living or dead, is entirely coincidental.

ISBN: 978-1-326-92810-0

PublishNation
www.publishnation.co.uk

FriendZone was first performed in 2012 as part of the Angelic Tales Season at The Theatre Royal Stratford East, Directed by Rikki Beadle Blair. Produced by Team Angelica, Rikki Beadle Blair and John R Gordon. The original cast were as follows:

Matt played by David Proud
Pete played by Jason Maza
Jaz played by Ashley Kumar
Amber played by Samantha Lyden
Candy played by Vanessa Carr
Ellen played by Vanessa Mayfield

Dedicated to Darrel Fox, Michael Hall, Matt Coleman, Matt Hodson, Pep Merola, and Bav Gela, your comic dialogue and enduring friendship made this possible.

Cast of Characters

Matthew	Matt to his friends. A bright wheelchair user in his 20's. Hopeless Romantic
Pete	Matt's Best friend, Commitment Phobic living with Amber.
Jaz	Matt's other friend. Works at River Island. Lady's man.
Amber	The better half of Pete, best friends with Ellen. Feisty but nice.
Ellen	School Teacher and searching for love. A china doll princess with a good sense of humour.
Candy	Works behind the Bar at Toho's. Appears dizzy but there is more than meets the eye.
Hooded Youth	A Hooded Youth (Played by same actor as Pete or Jaz)

Act One

Scene One	Toho's Bar
Scene Two	Matt's Flat
Scene Three	Amber and Pete's House
Scene Four	London Embankment

Act Two

Scene One	Amber and Pete's House
Scene Two	Darkness
Scene Three	Matt's Flat
Scene Four	Matt's Flat
Scene Five	Toho's Bar
Scene Six	Matt's Flat
Scene Seven	London Street

Act Three

Scene One	Toho's Bar
Scene Two	Matt's Flat
Scene Three	Amber and Pete's House
Scene Four	Amber and Pete's House
Scene Five	London Street

ACT

Scene 1 Toho's Bar

Toho's is a dank dark bar on a quiet street in London. It is a shadow of its former glory. A couple of sofas provide sanctuary for lost souls. A lone barmaid sits reading a book as our guys enter.

Matt, Jaz and Pete enter and greet the place like home.

PETE
It's just a little odd seeing my future sister-in-law whip it out in my living room when I'm trying to watch a film.

MATT
She's feeding a baby Pete, it's not meant to be a sexual experience for you.

PETE
No, I'm not saying it was, she has got nice... you know? I just didn't know where to look.

JAZ
Also, correct me if I am wrong but to be your future sister in law you would have to actually marry Amber.

PETE

Don't even! [go there] ...cos of her sister, she now wants one...we were in Mothercare the other day getting a gift for the baby and I'm sure I actually felt my testicles retract into my body. Scary shit.

(He looks at Matt)

Anyway McLovin, you've had a smile on your face all night, who is she?

JAZ

Believe me Pete you don't want to know. Prepare to lose at least an hour of your life mate.

MATT

Thanks Jaz, I'm not that bad. Well you know Ellen finally split up from Dominic...I kinda asked her out on a date and she said yes.

PETE

Oh fucking hell.

JAZ

Innit.

MATT

What? I've fancied her for five years! I thought you'd be pleased.

PETE

No I am, it's just what you need Matt, yet another friend.

MATT

What's that supposed to mean?

JAZ

I'm with Pete on this. You'll take her out fall in love straight away, she'll love the attention, you won't make a move and before you know it you're in the friend zone. I've never known a bloke who is so good at opening with a girl, you get digits faster than Hugh Hefner. You just can't close... you couldn't close a patio door.

MATT

Harsh.

PETE

But true.

MATT

But this is different, I've liked her for ages.

JAZ

Then you have to not be you... I mean be you...but don't be you... if you're you it won't work.

MATT

That makes sense...

PETE

I think what Jaz is trying to say is don't be her friend. You got to lock this down in the first few dates.

JAZ

Three actually.

MATT

Three?

JAZ

Yep scientific fact that if you're not attached to her face by the third date it ain't gunna happen.

PETE

She does know it's a date doesn't she?... You did say the word date?

MATT

Errr well...I just said about catching up over a meal.

(Jaz and Pete groan)

PETE

Doomed.

MATT

What was I meant to say?

PETE

Mate I catch up with my nan. She makes me a cuppa and gives me a biscuit. You don't want to go in there with that attitude trust me.

JAZ

Pete's right although don't trust him that much. Last time he was back in the game we were all doing the Macarena. Matt do you like this girl?

MATT

Is the Pope Catholic?

(Jaz is confused)

He is catholic, Jaz.

JAZ

Then repeat after me. I Matt Hodson.

MATT

I Matt Hodson.

JAZ

Will not be friends with this girl.

MATT

But I'm already friends with her.

JAZ

Then you're going to get screwed, just not in the way you hope. Look I'll get the drinks and then we are sorting out the game plan.

(Jaz looks to the bar)

Hello lads, new girl at the bar.

(The lads look as Candy gets up and cleans part of the bar)

PETE

Wow, how did we miss that?

MATT

Why would she work here? It's a shit hole.

JAZ

Her arse is like a peach.

PETE

Well you know what they say, five a day and all that....

JAZ

Matt, prepare for a lesson in the game.

(Jaz heads to the bar doing a cocky walk and almost falls over. He recovers and goes in for the kill. Smooth voice)

JAZ

Hi, Oh I see you are reading.

(Looking at the title we see the agony in his face)

Nitchay.

(She comes over and smiles)

CANDY

Don't you mean Nietzsche? (neecha).

(Jaz is dead in the water. Recovers. Goes back to talking normal)

JAZ

Yeah but Indian people pronounce it different.

(He is struggling)

Nitchay is my boi, just wish I could be like him.

CANDY

You want to live with your sister and mum and die of syphilis?

JAZ

I was thinking on a metaphalical level.

CANDY

Nice try handsome.

JAZ

I'm just not a pretty face.

CANDY

You mean you're not just a pretty face?

JAZ

Thank you.

(She giggles)

CANDY

So Einstein where do you work?

JAZ

Err...retail mostly... generally within the sector of... commerce... distribution... specifically River Island. And what brings you here?

CANDY

The tube normally.

(He forces a laugh and tries get the lads in on it)

JAZ

Wow that was quick... Am I disturbing your quality time with Nitchay?

(She giggles)

CANDY

It's OK he can wait. What you having?

JAZ

Three beers please. I'm Jaz.

CANDY

Candy.

JAZ

Wow that's a cool name.

CANDY

It's actually Candice but when I was a girl I couldn't spell it so everyone called me Candy. I've even got it on a necklace look.

(She shoves her sizable chest in his face. Pete and Matt are enjoying the show. Amber and

Ellen have walked in to
witness this)

JAZ

That's...

PETE

Amazing...

(Amber heads for the
lads, pissed)

AMBER

Er hello?

PETE

Alright babe.

AMBER

Don't alright babe me Pete, is it so hard to remember to buy toilet roll?

PETE

Oh shit yeah sorry, slipped my mind, got playing Call of Duty.

AMBER

For fuck sake Pete, how old are you?

(Pete doesn't get it)

PETE

How old you want me to be?...

(Amber storms off to the bar as Jaz comes back. Ellen is finishing her angry call)

PETE
(To Amber)
Love you...
(To Himself)
What a fucking bitch.

ELLEN
(Loud but cute into phone)
Well just so you know I've already replaced you with something far better. It cost 45 quid from Ann Summers and reminds me of Easter!!!!!!!!!!!!!...

(The boys have been listening. She is a little embarrassed)
Ooops, sorry.

JAZ
That's OK Ellen, but if you need batteries Boots have them on 3 for 2.

ELLEN
Thanks.

MATT
Was that Dominic? Your Ex?

ELLEN

Yeah.

MATT

You OK?

(She doesn't want to chat in front of the lads)

ELLEN

Chat about it later, you still OK for Saturday?

MATT

Yeah.

ELLEN

See you then, better go....

(She runs after Amber)

JAZ

She's wearing Channel Mademoiselle?

MATT

She always does, classy.

JAZ

Mark of a fine woman.

PETE

Er hello? Are we really gunna sit here and talk about perfume.

MATT

You alright?

(sarcastic)

Not like Amber to go off on one.

PETE

She's pissed cos I don't want to borrow 50 grand off her bitch of a mum to buy a house.

JAZ

Why don't you?

PETE

Cos it will feel like she owns me. I hate her. If Amber turns out like her I'm gunna kill myself.

MATT

She could end up like her Dad?

PETE

That's even worse......he supports Arsenal.

MATT

(To Jaz)

How did it go with Princess Peach?

JAZ

Swapped numbers, seed has been planted. Now just have to water the seed until I get to see the bush.

PETE

So, let's get Batman's game plan sorted. How are you going to avoid the friend zone. Jaz thoughts?

JAZ

Well you have just three dates to plant one on her, so you gotta take the lead. You don't want to know about her ex.

PETE

You don't care how her day was.

(Matt gets his phone out)

JAZ

You gotta play the smart game. When she texts, leave it half hour, if she calls even if you're by the phone let it go to voice mail. If she says she wants to go out Saturday, suggest Sunday and don't say why.

PETE

Never ask if she is OK!

(Pete clocks it)

Matthew, are you texting her now?

(He has been caught)

MATT
(Lying)
No

JAZ
Do you want to get laid or played Matthew? Now what do we know about her?

MATT
She is amazing, she's got great banter, she is mean to me. A proper princess and so cute.

PETE
See it's happening already, you're in love and you ain't even shared a prawn cocktail with the girl.

MATT
I'm sorry she just...takes my breath away.

JAZ
Oh dear god, and did you say she was cute?

PETE

You better hope she never calls you cute. Jaz tell him about the "C" Bomb?

JAZ

Ohhhh yeah. Dodge the "C" bomb at all costs.

MATT

The what?

JAZ

The most offensive four letter "c" word in the English language... "Cute." She calls you cute, end game.

PETE

The Muppets are cute.

JAZ

And how much poontang do you think Kermit gets? He fucks a pig!

MATT

But I like cute girls. Hot girls are hot but cute ones are cuuuuuuuute. First time we met, it was at Amber's Birthday. I remember having a drunken conversation about the best thing in the world being a woman holding cake, combines my two best things ever. Next day she turned up with a little cupcake in tin foil. I could have proposed there and then. She'd made it herself and everything. First girl to ever have cooked me cake.

(Pete and Jaz look shocked)

JAZ
You've had a five-year crush on a bird cos she made you a cupcake?

PETE
I really worry about your mental state Mathew, I really do.

JAZ
So, keep it in your head three dates, one, two, three, bosh. Got it.

MATT
No, if she is going to like me she is going to like me, not me trying to be you, or him.

(They spell it out for him)

JAZ/PETE
One, two, three, bosh!

Fade to black:

Scene 2 Matt's Flat

Matt's flat is stylish and minimal.

Matt and Ellen mid giggle enter. Ellen is a little too drunk and loud.

MATT

Once I talk about my testicles there is no going back.

ELLEN

Spill Mr H.

MATT

In my bathroom there is a little plastic seat I use in the shower and it has three holes in it to drain the water away. So I'm there having a shower and I hadn't noticed one of my boys had slipped nicely into the crack, for want of a better phrase.

ELLEN

No!

MATT

Yep. Went to stand up. I swear my uncle who lives in Coventry heard me scream.

ELLEN

You really are special aren't you.

MATT

Yep! More wine?

ELLEN

Why stop now eh?

(She takes in his flat and gets comfortable on the sofa. Matt gets a bottle and heads over)

Nice place Matt.

MATT

Thanks, trying to keep it that way but since Jaz moved in I feel like his dad.

(Jaz enters holding a large book)

Speak of the devil.

(Jaz is in his own little world)

JAZ

Evening.

MATT

What are you reading?

JAZ

It's a theasourus. Trying to increase my vo..vo... well say more big words.

ELLEN

Well you could start by calling it a thesaurus. It isn't a type of dinosaur.

JAZ

Thesaurus right got it.

MATT

You studying for your date with Candy?

JAZ

Yeah meeting her when she finishes work. Don't mind me carry on with your conversation.

(Jaz is getting some bits together. Slight awkwardness with him in the room)

ELLEN

Dominic phoned again earlier.

MATT

Your Ex?

ELLEN

Yes.

(Jaz looks daggers at Matt, Matt clocks it)

(Slight pause)

MATT
You OK?

ELLEN
Yeah.

MATT
Do you think you will stay friends?

(Jaz walks passed Matt and smacks him on the head with the Thesaurus. Ellen sees it and thinks it's a little odd
Jaz has picked up a marker for a white board and is now writing One, Two, Three, Bosh on the board)

ELLEN
No definitely not.

(She spots what he is doing)

What are you writing Jaz?

JAZ

This Ellen is a social experiment into the male mind.

ELLEN

Sound's interesting, what's it about?

JAZ

Well Ellen it's complicated but lets just say if it goes wrong you may never know. Anyway I'm outa hear. Matt, remember we spoke about that game? In the game the player was caught off side, got between the goal and the defender and lost possession? Just wanted to remind you of it.

(He crosses a line through the One)

MATT

Goodnight Jaz.

JAZ

Laters.

(He leaves)

ELLEN

Is he OK? he seems really weird tonight.

MATT

His cheese is falling off its cracker.

(Ellen is knocking back the wine. She gets up to put a track of music on. She presses play on an ipod on his side. It plays quietly)

ELLEN

Ooohh cool you got that album I told you about.

MATT

So you were saying your brother plays football?

ELLEN

Yes just round the corner actually, am at his game tomorrow morning...well, later this morning you know what I mean. Methinks I will a little hangover tomorrow Matthew.

MATT

You could always stay? More wine?

ELLEN

You trying to get me drunk because it's really working.

MATT

It's all part of the package.

ELLEN

That meal was looooovely. Those mussels were gorgeous. Thank you, we should have done this ages ago. You know for a geek your very cool, kinda cute.

(The "c" bomb has landed)

MATT

A cute geek?

ELLEN

Don't hide from who you are Matt, I've seen you wearing a Danger Mouse T - shirt.

MATT

Don't dis the Danger Mouse.

(They share a moment of smiling at teach other intently. They move closer. We think they are about to kiss. Ellen goes white)

Ellen

I think I'm going to be sick.

(She runs to the direction of the

bathroom. Matt hastily
chases her)

ELLEN (V.O)
Matt could you hold my hair?

(He looks horrified)

MATT
(sotto)
OK

Snap to black:

Scene 3 Amber and Pete's House

The house is nice and neat, very colourful.

The boys are all on the sofa.

PETE

How did holding her hair while she vomits fit the no friend zone plan?

MATT

I just thought If I got her a little drunk it might get us in the mood.

(Matt moves his feet and Pete notices his shoes)

PETE

Take your shoes off Matt.

MATT

I'm on wheels!

PETE

If Amber see's you with your shoes on in the house it's my bollocks.

(He takes them off)

JAZ

Feeding a woman fish and giving her wine is a rookie mistake, and stop talking about her ex!!!!!

MATT

Fair enough but I'm still not playing your game.

JAZ

If you don't play the game you'll get played. Women mind fuck you with their varge. Follow the rules or you'll be back to having a cozy night in watching Babestation.

PETE

It's rare but Jaz is talking sense, women never say what they mean. You have no choice, you're in a game from the minute you say Hello.

MATT

Ellen wouldn't play me.

(to Pete)

You know he wrote one two three bosh on my white board? In front of her!

PETE

(To Jaz)

Well done son.

MATT

Why does it have to be some elaborate game, can I not just be me?

JAZ/PETE

No.

PETE

Few reasons for that studly. Angela, Amy, Reena,

JAZ

Don't forget Becky.

PETE

Oh yes, Becky of course, and that bird from John Lewis that talked him into buying 150 quids worth of sheets and then never called him...

JAZ

Samantha...

PETE

That's the one, mate it's the same drill different day. You have that many coffee loyalty cards Columbia has stopped trading in coke. You meet a different female "friend" for coffee every day of the week.

MATT

But their friends.

(Pete and Jaz grown)

PETE

They are now but sit there and tell me you didn't start off wanting to sleep with them. I'm telling you two more dates and then that's it, friend zone. Play the game.

(No reaction from Matt)

JAZ

He's right bro.

(Amber enters. She has a coat on)

AMBER

Can you two please stop winding Matt up, can hear you upstairs.

(Matt wants the ground to swallow up)

MATT

Shit Bambi...so you...I mean you know I?......

AMBER

Don't worry Matt your secret is safe with me, although I think half of London knows you like her.

MATT

Does? [she].......

AMBER

No your fine, Ellen is a little clueless when it comes to that, you'd need to hoist a sign over the Olympic stadium for her to get the message.

(She goes over to him)

Look I know you properly like her so just see how it goes yeah. Try not to make her vomit next time though, and don't listen to these guys. See you children later.

(Pete gets a score from his pocket)

PETE

Here babe, have fun with the girls on me.

(Amber takes a score and kisses him she leaves)

Love you Princess... What a fucking bitch.

MATT

Pete!

PETE

No hear me out. So you know she asked me to get toilet roll and I didn't and she had a pop?

JAZ

Yeah the other night.

PETE

Well that ain't the half, so I'm sat up there this morning minding my own you know... ain't gunna draw you a diagram, gets to the end and she's only hid the toilet roll.

MATT

Mean.

PETE

Gets worse, I look round and she's hid the towels the flannels the lot, not a fucking thing to wipe my arse on. Then I see it don't I. Hasn't left me totally in the lurch. Sat there on the radiator pride of place is my West Ham top. First time in my life I have wanted to own a Millwall shirt. What a bitch.

Fade to black:

Scene 4 London Embankment

As Ellen and Matt walk slowly onto stage we see the glow of evening lights of the Thames. There is a small bench mid stage.

ELLEN

Almost finished but I need to go to Hamley's and it's going to be hell on earth at Christmas.

(We can hear the distant sound of music begins it is a soloist/band playing "Moonlight Serenade")

Oh Matt I love this song.

(Matt stops and holds out his hand)

MATT

Would you do me the honour.

(She takes it and he starts to dance with her. Spinning round and spinning her round. She giggles. This is a magical moment for them. Hand in hand they dance to the music looking at each other. After a few nice moments they face each other, holding both hands)

Happy Christmas Ellen.

(She beams)

ELLEN

Happy Christmas Matt.

MATT

I've got something to tell you.

(He heads over to the bench and sits on it. We think he is going to tell her. She follows)

ELLEN

Oh what?

(He hold the silence for a moment building it up)

MATT

I haven't got you a Christmas present yet.

ELLEN

Well just so you know, nothing says Happy Christmas more than Tiffany's.

MATT
Oh really. Might have to sell a kidney.

ELLEN
It will be so worth it.

MATT
For you maybe, I could die in the process.

ELLEN
I'm completely fine with that.

MATT
You’re so cruel to me.

ELLEN
Yep and you love it. You could always do something instead of buy me something?

MATT
Where are you going with this?

ELLEN
My laptop is broken Mr IT genius. I spilt wine on it and now I have to smack the 'B' Button.

MATT
Ha, well done. No promises I can fix it, but I'll have a look.

ELLEN

You're so cute.......Thanks for taking me to Somerset house.

MATT

I thought you were going to need a penguin to skate with.

ELLEN

Glad I had your hand. I went there once my ex.

MATT

What Harry?

ELLEN

No Ben.

ELLEN

(She giggles)

We'd been going out for a while and we just had never, you know... well he organized this romantic night taking me there and we had a meal and everything and he lived with his parents. We were both young. He was actually going to be my first.

MATT

What happened.

ELLEN

Well we got back to his and to mask the sound of what we were going to do he put on a mix tape. It was all OK but the moment he came over to kiss me it suddenly cut into "Tragedy" you know the Steps version. We both started laughing and the moment was gone. Such bad taste in music.

MATT

Bit hard to get freaky to the Steps.

(Slight silence)

Can I ask you something?

ELLEN

That's a very stupid question as you just did.

(He plucks up courage)

MATT

What do you think to the idea of...

(From nowhere a hooded youth runs up to them holding what looks to be a knife. He is trying to mug them quietly)

YOUTH

Give me your fucking money.

ELLEN
Are you serious? In my own city? You look young enough to be one of my students.

YOUTH
Just give me your fucking money.

(To Matt)
And yours...

MATT
Ellen let's not mess about just give him it.

YOUTH
You haven't got one of those disabled parking badges have you blud?

MATT
I don't carry it round with me.

(He kisses his teeth)
She gets her purse out. The youth spots a ring she is wearing.

YOUTH
That too sket.

(Ellen seems more upset about the idea of the ring going)

ELLEN

Don't be ridiculous. What on earth are you going to do with this? Do you know anyone that deals with diamonds in your endz or manor? Do you? And don't call me a sket.

YOUTH

(To Matt)

Should put a leash on that bitch of yours blud.

MATT

Now wait a minute...look just take my wallet and go, leave the ring alone.

YOUTH

You don't fucking say what I gets and don't ya get me.

(He takes the wallet and purse. Matt gets between him and Ellen)

Give me the fucking ring yeah.

(Matt gets between them and pushes the youth the youth pushes Matt really hard and he falls backwards out of his chair. The chair goes flying up and Matt

is laying on his back.
The youth runs)

MATT

Son of a...

ELLEN

Oh my god Matt are you OK?

(Matt holds his head)

Ellen gets his chair and he gets back in.

MATT

Please tell me that was your Nans ring or something?

(Pause)

ELLEN

Dominic got it for me. But it is from Tiffany's.

MATT

For fucks sake. I'd rather have sold a kidney...

ELLEN

You OK?

MATT

I've never been mugged before.

ELLEN

Let’s get you home, I'll call the Police. Get you some ice. Oh shit! That had my boots card in it.

(He looks puzzled)

Was going to use the points for a new hair dryer.

MATT

He's just had it away the the half chicken I had on my Nandos card too.

ELLEN

Come on let’s get something for your head.

MATT

Ellen, I'm sorry.

ELLEN

What for?

MATT

I think tonight I'm going to be sick.

Act 2

Scene 1 Amber and Pete's House

Amber is busy putting dips into a bowl. Pete is sat on the Sofa watching TV.

AMBER

Bit of help would be good Pete. they'll be arriving soon.

PETE

Babe, I'm on it...just gunna watch the end bit of this.

AMBER

Pete!

PETE

Babe it's my Birthday.

AMBER

How many times have you pulled the Birthday card today.

PETE

It's once a year and you know you love me.

AMBER

Debatable. So what's the situation with Jaz and Candy?

(He doesn't respond he is watching the TV)

AMBER

PETE!

PETE

What babe?

AMBER

Your mate, Jaz, is he with this girl or?...

PETE

Oh right yeah they are just friends with benefits at the moment but he's sniffing round for more.

AMBER

Really? Jaz actually wants a relationship? So tonight's not going to be awkward at all.

(Pete rolls his eyes, trying to watch the TV is pointless. He gets up and helps get the place ready)

PETE

Don't forget we also have Matt trying to chirpse Ellen.

AMBER

We need to get new friends.

(There is a knock at the door and Jaz enters with Candy, she is a little nervous)

JAZ

Evening.

AMBER/PETE

Hi

PETE

Shoes, Jaz, shoes.

(Jaz and Candy take their shoes off. There is a little awkward pause)

AMBER

You going to introduce us then Jaz?

JAZ

Oh yeah sorry this is Candy

CANDY

Lovely to meet you properly, I don't get chance to chat much in the bar.

AMBER

I don't know how you put up with this lot, I'm Amber.

CANDY

Hi.

(Candy heads over to Pete handing him a bottle of wine wrapped up)

CANDY

And you must be Phil.

PETE

Pete

CANDY

Oh sorry, Pete, I'm really bad with names.

AMBER

If you're stuck I have trained him to answer to dickhead.

CANDY

Ha, like it.

AMBER

Fancy a drink sweet heart?

CANDY

I'd love one.

AMBER

Wine?

CANDY

Nice.

(Amber pours some from a bottle on the table. Slight awkward silence.

CANDY

Lovely place, how long you been here?

AMBER

A few years, I want to move but he is taking some persuading.

PETE

Babe, we've talked about this and that place you wanted was too far away.

CANDY

Was it out of London?

AMBER

He means that it is too far from West Ham's stadium.

PETE

I'm just thinking of you babe, if it takes an extra half an hour each way I'll be gone for a whole hour more.

AMBER

(To Candy)

He says that as though it's a bad thing.

(Candy and Amber giggle)

CANDY

Men and football. Why do you want to move this place is lovely?

AMBER

It is but not big enough for a family so eventually we would have to move. I'd just rather do it now and get the place we really want.

CANDY

Oh that's so lovely you are thinking about a family already.

AMBER

Well I spend my days looking after this big kid.

(She points at Pete)

PETE

Thanks

AMBER

Jaz was telling us about Toho's, sorry about your job.

CANDY

Oh thanks, it's OK. I've only been working there while I do my degree.

PETE

You have a degree?

(Jaz and Amber glare at him)

CANDY

Well I will do soon, in my last year an everything.

PETE

Wow, that in some kind of beauty or dance thing?

CANDY

P.P.E

PETE

Nice one that will keep you fit, what's your favourite sport?

CANDY

No its not PE, It's Philosophy, Politics and Economics.

PETE

Yeah so not much running in that then...

JAZ
Brains and beauty.

CANDY
Awww thanks babe.

(She gives him a little kiss. He searches his memory for the next line)

JAZ
"A thing of beauty is a joy forever: its loveliness increases; it will never pass into nothingness." That's John Keats that is.

(Tumbleweed moment. They look at him)

PETE
So when does the bar shut?

CANDY
End of January. You all should come in as I've started giving all the drinks away when my boss isn't there.

PETE
Sounds brilliant.

JAZ
What's the plan for tonight?

AMBER

Well we thought few drinks here and maybe a wander into town.

CANDY

Amber how is my eyeliner? I had to do it on the tube, is it OK? I bet I look horrific.

AMBER

Don't be daft babe you look gorgeous. Have you seen the state of me? You caught me in the middle of getting ready.

CANDY

Really you look amazing.

AMBER

Shut up you look amazing. Got this amazing new bronzer. Grab that bottle and I'll show you.

(Candy smiles nicely grabs a bottle of wine and the girls leave)

PETE

(Sarcastic)

Amazing.

JAZ

So?...

PETE

What?

JAZ

What do you think?

PETE

Yes she seems nice mate. Trust you to find the most intelligent blonde in London.

JAZ

That's my problem... how do I stop her getting bored?

PETE

Want me to paint you a picture on that?

JAZ

No not like that the sex is fine it's just, went for coffee the other day and I got chatting and she started quoting all these ancient philosophers. I felt like a right tit. I thought Pluto was a Disney character but apparently, he is a philosopher. Mate, I've been up till midnight reading all kinds of books. I'm fucking knackered. Matt came in my room the other night as I was talking in my sleep, mate I was quoting Shakespeare!

PETE

If you need advice on spending time with a hot girl and talking to her instead of having sex with her, to be fair Matt is your guy....

JAZ

I'm thinking of maybe doing a course or something, show her I'm not thick. What do you think?

PETE

Not sure any places do a BA Honours in being a Twat but you can always ask.

JAZ

Not only that but you know?...

PETE

What?

JAZ

She's not Indian.

PETE

(Sarcastic)

Fuck off? Really?

JAZ

Piss off, it's just always thought I would settle down with you know, someone from my back ground.

PETE

So, date her for a bit. Nothing saying you have to have a long-lasting thing with her.

JAZ

But I kinda want too, never felt like it before, I can't get enough of her but then I feel like I shouldn't want to be with her. Then I think what the hell is she doing with me. What am I going to do?

PETE

Not even sure Jeremy Kyle could keep up with that one mate. Why is it everyone asks me? What do I know?

JAZ

You're living with one and you get it regularly.

PETE

Don't confuse the two, yes I live with one, but it ain't regular trust me....

(Matt comes launching into the house)

MATT

Evening,

PETE/JAZ

Alright.

MATT

Sorry I am late just got caught up. Happy Birthday mate.

(He hands him a GAME bag. He looks into it)

PETE

This the new Fifa?

MATT

Yep, just don't tell Bambi.

PETE

Fucking love you.

(Pete gives Matt a little hug)

Last shot, date three next, did you really take her to Somerset House?

MATT

Yes.

PETE

Did you take your own skates?

(Matt sticks his finger up at Pete)

MATT

It was romantic until we got mugged. Did you see me on BBC news?

PETE

Yes you Muppet, they really went to town on it.

JAZ

They got the headline slightly wrong, they said "Disabled man gets mugged". Should have been "Disabled man is a mug".

MATT

Thanks Jaz, thanks for that. You can both mock me, but Nandos sent me 100 quids worth of vouchers as I mentioned in the interview I lost my loyalty card.

PETE

When's your last date then?

MATT

Not my last date Pete, it's a marathon not a sprint. Having a meal at mine this week we thought it would be safer than going out. I'm cooking.

JAZ

I can't believe she's chucked up once, then you last time, and for date number three you are cooking. That's a one way ticket to an evening of chunder.

PETE

You going to wow her with cheesey beans on toast? Or a Chicago town microwave pizza?

JAZ

Forget the food you have to get the conversation onto sex, put on some good music, wear a better shirt, give her a massage or something.

MATT

It's starting to sound like the opening of a porn film. I've told you I am not playing your games. Never met anyone who I have felt such a connection with it's like we are perfectly balanced, left and right. Ying and Yang.

JAZ

That's lovely but it's about time you put your ying in her yang. I'm serious, no matter what happens you must achieve what I like to call... squelchy love.

PETE

Sorry did you just say squelchy love? Dunno bout Ellen but I think I'm going to throw up. Matt, he's wrong in the

head but he's right about the sex.
It's time to start slipping it in.

Fade to Black:

Scene 2 Darkness

We stay in darkness, smoke starts to engulf the stage. As they talk it gets worse.

Ellen (V.O)

Matt, are you sure that is meant to be that smokey?

Matt (V.O)

Small technical problem in the kitchen.

(Fire alarm sounds)

Could you get the fire alarm, I'm trying to find the window?

ELLEN (V.O)

I can't reach it, I'm too short.

MATT (V.O)

I never can either. Use the mop handle in the cupboard and smack it hard.

Scene 3 Matt's Flat

As the lights come up we see Matt and Ellen on the sofa, they are looking at two plates of cheesey bean juice and a broken Fire alarm on the table. The white board now has "two" with a line through.

ELLEN

Sorry about your fire alarm.

MATT

Sorry about your Beef Wellington......fucking Nigella Lawson.

ELLEN

Cheesey beans were nice though. Ten out of ten for effort on the Wellington Matt.

(Jaz enters holding Trivial Pursuit cards)

JAZ

Test me.

(He gives them to Matt. Matt picks a card)

MATT

OK what direction does the Leaning Tower of Piza Lean? North, West, South East or South West?

JAZ

How am I meant to know that?

ELLEN

Thought you were good with erections Jaz.

MATT

It's South East.

JAZ

Spent all night on them. Bollocks. You children going to be OK now if I leave, not going to torch the place again?

ELLEN

I will make sure he doesn't go near the cooker.

(Jaz goes over to the white board and draws a ring around the three)

How is your experiment going Jaz?

JAZ

Sadly it's nearing the end with no positive results as of yet.

MATT

Are you LEAVING?

JAZ

Yes, catch you kids later.

ELLEN

Bye

(He's gone)

He is a little odd isn't he. So you going to come out New Years?

MATT

I....I don't know maybe.

ELLEN

Oh come on it will be miles more fun with you there.

MATT

Will think about it. Wine?

ELLEN

Yes but only a little.

(Matt gets up to get a bottle)

You started writing that book yet?

(He shakes his head)

Matt! I told you carpe diem! I'm disappointed. Just get writing.

MATT

Thinking of a romantic comedy, then I think sci fi, but not sure.

ELLEN

Just pick one, it will be brilliant whatever you write.

(Ellen moves and pulls an uncomfortable face. She pulls a box of condoms from underneath her)

ELLEN

Matt, why is there a packet of JLS condoms on your sofa?

(Matt is mortified)

MATT

I'm going to kill him. Jaz must have left them.

(She goes to put them on the side)

ELLEN

And these ones? Also JLS.

(Matt even more mortified. She see's there is another packet on the side)

Aren't these too old to use now?

MATT

Yes and apparently they split.

ELLEN

Oh dear that was awful.

MATT

Can I come back to you when I think of a better punchline?

(She sits back on the sofa giggling)

Why can't things just run smooth?

ELLEN

What do you mean?

MATT

Elle, since we have been hanging out together I've taken you out for food poisoning, got you mugged, burnt your beef and made you sit on Aston Merrygold's something for the weekend. Hardly a great list.

ELLEN

Strange that I have kinda enjoyed it, apart from the vomit and mugging. You're not boring I'll give you that.

MATT
You've had fun?

ELLEN
Don't fish for a compliment Matthew, but yes. You're cute.

(Crushed the c bomb has arrived again, goes in for the kill)

MATT
Yeah thanks... look we need to talk...

(Fearing "the talk" and possible rejection. Ellen panics and cuts him off)

ELLEN
Oh me too.

MATT
Oh OK, well ladies first.

ELLEN
There is this guy I have known for ages and since I broke up with Dom I have spend more time chatting to him.

(Matt thinks she is talking about him)

MATT

OK.

ELLEN

Well, he asked me out this week on a proper date.

(Matt's world is crushed)

Is it too soon?

(Matt doesn't answer)

Just say if you think it's too soon?

MATT

I think if you want to go you should go.

(There is a knock at the door)

MATT

(At the door)

Go away!

(He turns back to Ellen)

PETE (V.O)

Matt it's Pete, mate let me in.

(Matt gets up and opens the door. Ellen looks down but Matt doesn't notice. We see Pete with a big bag in one hand and a pair of hair straighteners in the other)

MATT

You OK?

PETE

Amber kicked me out. She gone fucking mental.

(He comes in seeing Ellen)

Oh fuck sorry, I didn't know it was....

MATT

Doesn't matter, what happened?

PETE

We had a barney over that fucking house and she kicked me out. Said it's over. Like I give a fuck.

ELLEN

I better go see her.

(Ellen gets ready to leave)

MATT
OK, Elle er sorry, I'll call you bit later.

(She goes. As Matt crosses the room he pauses for a moment and puts a line through the "Three" on the white board.

MATT
What's with the straighteners.

PETE
She's hidden my Playstation, so I nicked em. An eye for an eye Matthew. This is going to be brilliant. Non-stop Call of Duty, pizza, beer. I can watch match of the day without having to talk about fucking scatter cushions.

(Pete does a funny cockney double time walk up and down the stage)

MATT

What are you doing?

PETE

This Matthew, is me wearing my shoes inside.

Snap to black:

Scene 4 Matt's Flat

Jaz is sat on the sofa reading more trivial pursuit cards..

Pete enters he is holding washing. Wearing yellow gloves.

PETE

I thought you said Candy is coming over?

JAZ

She is.

PETE

Have you seen your room?

JAZ

Yeah but the bed is clear.

PETE

Never mind the bed she's got to put up with that smell, when did you last change those sheets?

(No answer from Jaz)

Jaz!

JAZ

What?

PETE

You wanna go sort your room out? If the CSI lot shine a blue torch over your bed it will light up like Vegas.

JAZ

Nah man, there is some Fabreeze in the kitchen, will spray it down. It's all cool. Gotta memorize this stuff.

PETE

You know you've been at that all morning? you ain't even took the rubbish out. I've spent the last hour trying to work out what that smell in the fridge is, it's disgusting. Smells like my granddads feet. Sort your life out mate.

JAZ

Farking hell, no wonder Amber chucked you out.

(Candy knocks on the door)

PETE

Door.

(Pete goes into the bedroom. Jaz gets up to open the door. She pounces on him)

CANDY
OK, have got an hour for lunch and you're my snack.

(He tries to get a word in)

JAZ
Can...

CANDY
Don't talk just get naked.

(As she pushes him onto the sofa. Pete enters)

PETE
Sorry.

CANDY
Bloody hell! Jaz why didn't you say Pete was here?

JAZ
My mouth doesn't work with a tongue in it.

(He thinks about that)

With your tongue in it.

PETE
Er. So... awkward. Gunna nip to the shops... yeah... as you were.

(He leaves)

JAZ

By the way Pete is stopping.

CANDY

Ha, you're so funny.

(He goes to kiss her.
She pulls away)

Kinda ruined the mood now.

(He flirtatiously moves
over to her)

JAZ

Did you know that in Papua New Guinea there are over 850 indigenous languages?

CANDY

(Sarcastically)

Fascinating.

(He tries another
tactic)

JAZ

Anyway, was thinking of checking out the National Gallery at the weekend if you fancy it?

CANDY

The what?

JAZ

National Gallery and then I thought we would go to the Tate seminar on postermodism

CANDY

The what?

JAZ

So you don't fancy it?

CANDY

Hmmmm gee let me think, no.

JAZ

But it's cultural and all that.

CANDY

It's also boring as shit babe.

(Pause)

JAZ

Candy can I ask you something. Are we like… you know... a couple?

CANDY

Why label it Jaz? Can't we just have some fun?

JAZ

Yeah but...

CANDY

Shhh, I didn't come him for your conversation. Come on, let's drain some blood from that head of yours before you do anymore thinking.

(She leads him into his bedroom)

Candy V.O

Oh my god what's that smell?

Fade to black:

Scene 5 Toho's Bar

Toho's is empty, Matt is asleep on the sofa and Candy is behind the bar.

Jaz and Pete rush in they head over to Candy.

JAZ

Got your message where is he?

CANDY

Over there, been here for the best part of the afternoon.

PETE

Has he been drinking?

CANDY

Not that much but I didn't really know what to do so thought I'd text you. He's been sparko for a while.

JAZ

Cheers.

CANDY

I'm making him a coffee.

(They head over. Pete shakes him awake)

PETE
Mate you OK?
(He wakes)

MATT
What you doing here?

PETE
They don't normally allow people to fall asleep in bars Matthew, especially on New Years day.

JAZ
What the hell happened?

MATT
Milky fucking Joe.

JAZ
What?
(Candy comes over with a coffee. Matt gets up)

MATT
Milky Joe, last night she went to the New Years party with Milky Joe, they had a kiss at midnight and she's in love.

CANDY
Babe how'd you know this? Where you even there?

MATT

No she didn't text me happy new year. I text her this morning to ask about her night and she said it was amazing. She went to the party with this guy.

PETE

Didn't she invite you to the party?

MATT

In a flat on the 8th floor, without a lift. I didn't want to look like a prat in front of her so I said no.

PETE

Shit mate, but how'd you know his name and that they kissed?

MATT

I don't know they kissed but its New Years Eve, I'm normally so pissed I'd kiss Ann Widdecombe. I looked on facebook and she has a new friend. His name is fucking Milky Joe. What kind of a prick has a name called that!

CANDY

Oh babe I am sorry, little disturbed by the facebook stalking but it does all seem to add up.

PETE

Just cos she went with him to a party doesn't put you out of the game.

CANDY

Yeah but she told Matt about it, from a girl perspective you only do that to friends. If Matt was a potential she would keep it from him.

JAZ

See the three date rule is golden, didn't happen so now Matt's in the friend zone.

CANDY

Is that what you guys think? Just three dates? So I would only be worth three dates of effort Jaz?

JAZ

Babe, no, it's just we were trying to tell Matt to play the game a bit more. Don't matter now the games over.

PETE

Nah he's an outside bet but still a contender.

CANDY

Jaz is right now she has established Matt as a friend it's gunna be tricky to get him out of it.

MATT

HELLLO I am still in the room!

JAZ

Sorry mate.

CANDY

Look Matt, I'm impressed at the effort you have put in with her. It's kinda cute. Nobody has ever put in that mount of work for me.

(Jaz is gutted at this. He takes a trivial pursuit card from his pocket and rips it up)

If she contacts you give me a ring. I will try and help.

PETE

See there's hope, glass half full and all that.

JAZ

And you can trust her she has studied P.P.E

PETE

But dating a complete T.I.T.

(To Jaz)

That spells TIT

Snap to black:

Scene 6 Matt's Flat

Matt, Pete and Jaz arrive home.

MATT

Look at him Pete

(Matt gets out his phone and shows him a pick)

The guys wearing a trilby in his profile prick and is called Milky Joe for gods sake.

PETE

Mate, think you've got to move on.

MATT

You're right. What's the point? I'm just a friend, this guy is sweeping her off her feet and I'm left on the side, again. You know I grew up watching those shitty black and white movies where the girl runs after the guy in the rain and tells him she loves him. It's always in the rain. I just want some girl to do that to me.

PETE

Life isn't a film though mate. It ain't simple for me either, I'm sleeping on your sofa remember....

JAZ
And I'm convinced Candy is going to realize I'm a retard and leave me.

PETE
We sound like a right bunch. Life's just fucking shit.

MATT
Plus I got a parking ticket yesterday. Fucking traffic wardens. And I stubbed my toe on my bed this morning.

JAZ
Yeah but you can't feel it can you?

MATT
That's not the point! Shit just keeps happening to me.

JAZ
Oh I see where you were going with that.

(Pause)

MATT
I can't even picture my wedding. I get to the part where it's time for the first dance and the dream fades.

PETE
What's going on, you're never like this. Ever.

MATT

I wanted to be the man of her dreams. I couldn't even stop her getting mugged.

PETE

Anyone can get mugged, none of us are perfect. I hate my hair.

JAZ

I hate Pete's hair too.

PETE

Trying to make a point Jaz you don't have to celebrate it.

(Jaz nods as Matt smiles)

PETE

Mate, I know your hurting but you had three chances to tell her.

MATT

But did I Pete, really?

PETE

You ever thought that all those things happened for a reason, like fate. You never know you might not be meant to be with her cos of some fitty you are going to meet next week.

JAZ

Bro trust me, from a family of Hindu's. Everyone has a Dharma, a place in life. You just gotta accept yours just ain't going to be with her. I'd love to be you, you've got a perfect chat up line, shave your hair and give you a tan and say your back from Afghanistan. I would....

(Pete looks at Jaz)

PETE

Yeah....well......not going to go into exactly why that wouldn't work for you Jaz but admire your idea.

(Matt is tearful)

MATT

You know I've never ever felt like this. Not about anyone. I've never wanted to change who I am. I should have just crawled up there. I'd have been at that party. I'd have been with her. I've lost her.

PETE

You have a good connection with her but so, you'll have that again with someone else. I think you've just got to walk away.

MATT
That's the point though Pete, I can't walk away.

(Long Silence. For once the bravado is gone and Jaz and Pete are lost for words. There is a knock at the door)

That's Ellen.

PETE
How'd you know?

MATT
She always knocks like that.

(Jaz gets up and runs to the kitchen)

PETE
Where are you going?

JAZ
Chop an onion, Matt's eyes are red and she'll think that's why his crying.

PETE
Don't be daft.

(He opens the door and it's Amber)

AMBER

Hi can I chat to Pete.

MATT

Sure

(He turns to Pete)

See, for you life is a fucking film.

(Matt and Jaz stay)

AMBER

Pete, look I'm sorry I got so angry I just wanted to spend time with you. I wanted a boyfriend who is there Pete, not always playing games with people online. I wanted to know we were planning a future together. I didn't want to have to ask you 20 times to tidy up. I'm not trying to have a go I just want you to understand why I got so upset. I can be with a man who is obsessed with West Ham, I can even be with a man who thinks my mum's a bitch. I do too. I can't be with a boy who ignores me to play computer games.

(Small pause)

I know I'm hard work at times and I hear myself saying stuff to you and feel bad, especially in front of your mates because I love you.

That's all I wanted to say.

(He says nothing. She leaves)

JAZ

Who's up for a game of Fifa?

(Pete runs after Amber. They boys follow)

Snap to black:

Scene 7 London Street

As Amber walks across stage Pete gives chase. Matt and Jaz arrive as the action unfolds.

PETE

Amber

(He drops to his knees and she instantly melts)

AMBER

What are you doing?

PETE

No question it's you, you daft cow.

AMBER

No no no I pictured this in like Paris or something Pete....

PETE

Well I pictured it half time at London Stadium so let’s just crack on shall we... I can be with a woman who hates computer games. I can even be with a woman who rinses me in front of my mates. But just so you know if I ever have to wipe my arse on a West Ham top again it's end game. Amber, I know I am a complete twat, but I promise I

will always be your complete twat.
Amber will you marry me.

(She is now a little tearful)

AMBER

Yes.

(They kiss. Matt and Jaz high five)

Fade to black:

Act 3

Scene 1 Toho's Bar

The bar is in pieces. Boxes are about the place and what was once a nice bar is all but gone. Amber and Ellen sit on the sofa, joined by Pete and Jaz. Candy is packing up the bar area pottering onstage and off. They are all reminiscing looking at the bar.

PETE
Shame really innit. Could have had our wedding reception here.

AMBER
Please tell me you are joking or the wedding is off.

PETE
Babe, would I book your special day at a place like this.

AMBER/ELLEN
Yes

JAZ
Have to say I really am going to miss it.

PETE
Really, by the looks of it you're taking the best bit of it with you.

(He points to Candy.
Amber looks daggers at
him)

What? It's a compliment, it's not me being a perv.

ELLEN

Keep digging Pete.

AMBER

Why have we come here?

JAZ

Free booze.

PETE

And let it not be said I miss last orders anywhere!

ELLEN

Is Matt coming?

(Pete and Jaz look at
each other)

PETE

No he said he couldn't make it.

(Ellen looks upset and
Amber spots it)

ELLEN
Oh, doing anything fun?

(Pete and Jaz share another look)

JAZ
Dunno.

(It's slightly awkward)

I need to break the seal.

PETE
Me too.

(The boys get up to leave)

AMBER
Slightly worrying you are both going at the same time.

JAZ
Nothing like that Bambi.

AMBER
Oh I'm not worried, either way you will be back in two minutes.

(she gives a cheeky grin to Pete)

PETE

Harsh.

AMBER

True!

(Ellen seizes the moment of just them)

ELLEN

OK so what the hell is up with the Matt thing?

(Amber looks down)

Not you too! Why is it every time I mention him people change the subject?

AMBER

Have you spoke to him recently?

ELLEN

No, I've tried, he's just not texting back or picking up.

AMBER

No texts at all?

ELLEN

None. I don't know what I've done to upset him. I think he hates me.

AMBER

No Elle, Matt could never hate you. I...

ELLEN

What?

AMBER

No I really can't say.

(Candy comes over with drinks)

CANDY

OK ladies drinks are on me.

AMBER

Will he not notice?

CANDY

I don't care he is such a wanker.

ELLEN

Who are we talking about?

CANDY

My soon to be ex boss, tried to grab my ass yesterday the little perv.

(The boys return)

Guys, drinks are on me, and we have a load more to get through so go for it.

PETE
Sweet.

(Jaz raises his bottle)

JAZ
To friends!...oh no. To Pete and Amber and your engagement.

CANDY/ELLEN
Pete and Amber.

CANDY
Show me the ring again.

(Amber shows off an engagement ring)

CANDY
That's so lovely.

PETE
Now the Playstation is going, was thinking of getting Sky HD to fit in the gap? So you can watch all your favorite shows in all their glory.

AMBER
Why do I want to see The Only Way is Essex in high Definition? I might actually see the one brain cell in their head. You sure it's not for the footie?

PETE
Admittedly the football would also be high def but I was thinking more of you babe.

JAZ
Do you think if you watch Babestation in high def you might actually get to see their.....

(He stops mid sentence realizing what he is about to say. They are all stunned)

Anyways so let's toast to the happy couple yeah. To the beautiful Amber.

AMBER
Oh that's very sweet Jaz. You after a free Sunday lunch again?

(He nods)

Well if you want to come over Sunday, and Candy you are welcome too, Ellen and me are going to be looking at wedding stuff and places for the engagement party if you want to help?

(Ellen looks a little shocked that Amber is friendly with Candy)

CANDY
That sounds well nice. I love weddings that will be lovely.

ELLEN
So Candy, you going to find another bar to work in?

CANDY
No need to concentrate on my dissertation so going to look for something with better hours.

ELLEN
What are you studying?

CANDY
PPE.

PETE
(To Ellen)
That's nothing to do with sport.

ELLEN
What made you do that?

CANDY
Well I was born in India and my Dad moved us back here when I was a baby.

(Jaz and Pete share a "bosh" look re Indian birth)

He wanted me to be a teacher but I said fuck that I want to make something of my life, you know what they say "those that can't do, teach."

(All the guys look a little awkward)

You're a teacher?

ELLEN

Yep.

CANDY

Lovely... must be nice.

(Awkward pause)

PETE

Jaz, you up for one last Playstation session before it goes!

JAZ

Ah yeah but I'm gunna kick your ass, Matt sold me his console so I have been practicing.

PETE

What? He sold his Playstation? Why?

JAZ

He has started writing a book and said it was a distraction.

CANDY
Wow what's the book about?

PETE
Romance

JAZ
Or lack of....

(Ellen gets up really quickly and heads to the ladies. They all look)

PETE
Well done Jaz. So this isn't going to be an uncomfortable wedding at all.

(Amber goes after her)

I have no idea what to say to him.

JAZ
He hasn't left the house. He's almost grown a beard so you know he must have been home for weeks.

CANDY
Well, I could always try and chat to him. I like Matt he's a sweetie.

PETE
What you going to say to him?

CANDY
I have studied Aristotle, Freud and Plato I'm sure I can handle a bit of heartbreak.

JAZ
Bless. Babe, it's not Plato, it's Pluto.

Fade to black:

Scene 2 Matt's Flat

Candy is on the Sofa next to Matt. He is on the laptop. They are looking closely at something. A box of chocolates is being annihilated.

CANDY

How about that one?

MATT

Er maybe, I have never done red before?

CANDY

Or that one.

MATT

Yes! 100 percent yes. Browsing your Facebook for birds is not getting that program installed.

CANDY

Well babe, I know a lot of fit young girls and I would love to set you up. Now scroll to the F's.

MATT

Who am I looking at.

CANDY

Amy Farreli she is half Italian.

(Matt finds her)

MATT

Oh my god she is stunning. Does she want a new best friend?

(Candy chuckles)

CANDY

No more friends Matthew. Send her a message, I went to school with her and she is nice and works in the city.

(He passes her the laptop. Gets up to get a wine bottle)

MATT

I don't know, I think I may need more wine.

CANDY

I could send one for you?

MATT

"er hello Amy, yeah its Candice from school remember? so anyway was wondering if I could set you up with this geek".

CANDY

You are not a geek babe, everyone likes star wars, and you play the guitar and you're writing a book. I know your hurting over her but there is a famous quote which goes "In the end the love you take is equal to the love you make."

MATT

That some Philosopher?

CANDY

No, Lennon and McCartney, I'm shocked you didn't know that one as you are such a massive Beatles fan.

MATT

I just don't think I am ready yet. I think I just need time to just be me.

CANDY

But...

MATT

How can I look for someone if I am still trying to get her out of my head...

CANDY

Babe I...

MATT

Honestly it's fine. I'm just going to crack on with writing and just try not to over think everything.

CANDY
You trying to convince me or yourself there hun?

MATT
Healthy mix of both?

(He raises his glass)

To new friends and new beginnings.

CANDY
Well said.

MATT
You had your hair cut?

CANDY
Yes, I had it feathered.

MATT
Looks lovely.

CANDY
Thanks Matt, Jaz didn't even notice. He's been too busy thinking the foundation of western philosophy was written by a Disney dog.

(They stare at each other)

It's odd I feel like I have known you for years.

(Ellen knocks at Matt's door. Still smiling and with glass in hand he opens it. Ellen is stood there with a laptop bag and a bottle of wine)

MATT

Hi

ELLEN

Hi, can I come in?

MATT

Yes course.

(She enters and notices Candy)

ELLEN

Oh Hi.

CANDY

Hi.

ELLEN

I... I should have called but was in the area and thought you might be able to tackle my laptop.

MATT

That would have been great it's just I've got to install something on Candy's, it's likely to take a few hours.

ELLEN

Oh yeah that's fine we can do it another time maybe?

(Small pause)

You been OK? haven't really spoke in a while.

MATT

All good just started writing and stuff.

ELLEN

Great, well glad you're all OK and everything. I'll leave you too it. Just text me when you are free and we can have this bottle.

MATT

Sure.

ELLEN

See you later, bye Candy.

CANDY

Bye.

(She leaves. Matt sits on the sofa close to Candy)

CANDY

You OK babe?

(Matt is angry)

MATT

For fuck sake. Jaz and Pete are right. Three dates. No more fucking mates.

CANDY

Oh my god Matt don't think I have ever seen you angry. It suits you.

(He goes and sits back on the sofa)

MATT

Why is it to get a woman interested you have to act like you're not interested at all?

(They catch each other's eyes. She starts to talk softer)

CANDY

It's probably because if you can't have something you want it more.

(She moves closer)

Sometimes if you know you shouldn't it's the naughtiness that attracts you.

MATT

Naughty is attractive.

CANDY

I definitely like naughty.

(They are almost kissing. Matt pulls away)

MATT

Wow this is hard.

CANDY

Really? I hadn't even kissed you?

MATT

No not that! The situation is hard.

CANDY

Oh, ooops.

MATT

Six months ago I would have given my right arm and gone round in circles for life to kiss someone like you but…

CANDY

Ellen?

(Matt nods)

MATT

Jaz

(Candy nods)

CANDY

Jaz just he doesn't seem to get me, not like you, he just keeps coming out with weird shit. It's just really great sex. Whereas with you I can chat, and you get to park right next to the door in Westfields. Ellen is mad.

MATT

Thanks, that means a lot. You do realize Jaz is learning all that to impress you?

CANDY

Really?

MATT

He doesn't want to you to think he is dumb. He's even applied for a library card.

CANDY

Is that why?... Oh my god.

MATT

Just tell him he doesn't need too and I promise, you two are a perfect match.

CANDY

That's so sweet of you to tell me. Most men would have said anything to sleep with me.

MATT

I'm not most men, and Jaz is my boy, and you make him happy.

CANDY

OK well we still need to sort out you.

MATT

Let's give that friend of yours an email eh?

Fade to black:

Scene 3 Pete and Ambers house.

We are post Sunday lunch and there is some serious vegging out happening. Jaz and Candy, Matt and Ellen and Pete and Amber relax after the meal.

AMBER
Look, I don't want you going on your stag do the night before the wedding. You'll end up marrying Jaz in a kebab shop.

PETE
This last night of freedom isn't sounding too free.

AMBER
There has to be rules.

CANDY
No she's right I read it in a magazine. It's like you can have a stripper but not two.

ELLEN
Why would you want two strippers.

JAZ
Why would you not?

MATT
Don't worry, I will make sure he doesn't get up to too much trouble. I've got to head off.

(He gets ready to go)

AMBER
Really?

ELLEN
Why?

MATT
Oh just got to go meet someone.

CANDY
Good luck babes.

(She winks at him)

MATT
Thanks, Thanks for the dinner Amber. Pete, will look into Amsterdam it has great... er... canals.

(He makes the sign for smoking)

PETE
Liking the sound of that. Don't forget the big move Saturday.

AMBER

No Pete, Matt doesn't have to help us move.

PETE

Yes he does, I ain't having him pull the disabled card, me and Jaz were off work for a week with back pain after putting his wardrobes in. He can fucking well help.

MATT

It's true Bambi, I do owe him one. Plus I can order Chinese and make tea.

AMBER

OK well see you Saturday then.

(He nods at her)

MATT

Catch you guys later.

All

Bye

(He leaves)

AMBER

Right dumb and dumber, hit the kitchen, us girls have got to talk wedding stuff and colour schemes for the house.

PETE

Do we have too just now, football is bout to start.

AMBER

Ellen my period cramps are so bad this month.

ELLEN

Amber I have been gushing.

(Pete and Jaz look at each other)

PETE

Mate, I'll wash you dry.

JAZ

Deal.

(They leave as the girls giggle)

CANDY

Men are just too easy to control.

AMBER

Nice to see you and Matt back talking.

ELLEN

We are but it's not like before.

CANDY

He is so funny. He said the best thing the other day. We were out shopping in town and he...Oh what was it he said....

(Ellen is taken back)

ELLEN

You went shopping with Matt.

CANDY

Yeah then he took me to Jamie's Italian in town.

ELLEN

The one near Covent Garden?

CANDY

That's the one.

ELLEN

Oh OK.

CANDY

He's a good friend and I think people don't appreciate him enough.

ELLEN

Is that aimed at me?

CANDY
No, I wouldn't possibly aim that at anyone...I'm just saying, he's nice and people take advantage.

ELLEN
Like getting free meals at Jamie Olivers.

AMBER
Shall we look at dresses then?

Snap to Black:

Scene 4 Amber and Pete's house

We see the starts of chaos. Candy and Jaz are on the sofa getting frisky.

CANDY

Stop it.

JAZ

Fellatio.

CANDY

Stop it...

JAZ

Coitus. Copulation

CANDY

God I love it when you talk smart dirty to me.

JAZ

The thesaurus has some use. Fornication!

CANDY

I can talk smart dirty too. When I get you home I am going to.

(She whispers in his ear. He gets his phone out to look it up)

Don't google it, trust me you'll like it. After you made me pass out during sex last night it's the least I can do, almost had to borrow Matt's chair this morning I couldn't walk.

(Amber and Pete have come in mid sentence although Candy didn't know)

PETE

Er we could come back if?...

AMBER

No Pete...you need to stay and learn by the sounds of it.

PETE

(To Amber smiling)

What a bitch.

(He gives her a massive kiss. Ellen comes in)

ELLEN

Howdy.

AMBER

Welcome to chaos Elle. Oh my god I don't know where to start.

PETE

Don't look at me you're the one who wanted to move.

AMBER

Right so Pete and Jaz, come with me you can get the suitcases down and we can fill them up.

(Pete, Amber and Jaz leave. Ellen is left with Candy. Awkward silence)

CANDY

How's school?

ELLEN

Good thanks. You get your laptop sorted?

CANDY

Yeah he is a genius.

(Silence)

ELLEN

How's Uni?

CANDY

Good just a lot of work.

(Silence. Matt enters)

MATT

Hiya.

ELLEN

Hi Matt.

CANDY

Hey McLovin.

(He laughs)

MATT

You have to stop calling me that.

ELLEN

Am I missing something?

MATT

It's from the film Superbad, little in joke.

(Amber comes in followed by Pete and Jaz holding massive suitcases, they dump them on the floor)

AMBER

Hi Matt. Welcome to the madhouse.

(Matt heads over to Candy to whisper something at her. Ellen spots it)

ELLEN

Right enough! What's going on between you two?

(Jaz looks around)

MATT

What?

(Everyone stops)

ELLEN

You looked pretty damn cosy the other night.

JAZ

What?

MATT

Mate, let me explain I was installing that program and you knew she was over.

CANDY

You calling me a slut?

ELLEN

You're the educated one "babe" you figure it out.

CANDY

I don't think you want to pick an argument with me, you're out matched "babe". As a wise man once said "No one is a friend to his friend, who does not love in return." So Matt's worth my attention and "Good actions give strength to ourselves, and inspire good actions in others". So I will be as nice to him as I like....

JAZ
She ain't quoting Disney.

MATT
Candy it's OK just calm down. Ellen what on earth is wrong with you?

ELLEN
You are being off with me and I want to know why?

MATT
I'm not Ellen.

ELLEN
Why have you stopped texting and calling?

MATT
We're friends Ellen, I...

ELLEN
No Bullshit, it appears that you told everyone we know that you liked me EXCEPT ME! And now you and Candy are all pally pally on you are taking her

to Jamie's and I'm not even worth a text message.

MATT

Does it even matter? you met someone.

ELLEN

No, I shared a drunken new year kiss with a jerk called Milky Joe and then threw up in his hat. It's not my fault you never asked me how I felt about you. It's not fair and I want things back the way they were.

MATT

Ellen, I... I can't be the guy who picks you up when another guy knocks you down. I just can't go through that again.

ELLEN

Matt, I've never asked you to do that.

(She gets tearful)

I don't want you to be my friend, I want... it scares me but I want to maybe think about more than that.

(Long pause)

MATT

You don't have to say that Ellen, I know I come with too much baggage. I want more for you, and I'd need more from you.

ELLEN
(Gentle)
You talking about your chair?

MATT
Well yes but...

ELLEN
Don't be stupid. Every man needs fixing, none of you are perfect, it's part of the fun of a new relationship, we get to alter the bits we don't like. With you it's your taste in clothes not your chair. How many times did I tell you you were cute Matt? I couldn't have dropped more hints. And I tell you about a guy and instead of going jealous you tell me to date him! Look if you liked me enough you wouldn't let your issues get in the way. You'd man up and tell me.

(Pause)

Do you like me Matt?

(He says nothing. She leaves. He looks to Pete and Jaz. He goes after her. They all follow

<u>Scene 5 Street</u>

On a London Street in the rain.

Ellen walks onto stage and Matt chases her.

MATT

Ellen wait...

(As she stops and turns Pete, Jaz, Candy and Amber catch them up. Matt turns to see them all, then turns back to Ellen)

ELLEN

What Matt?

MATT

OK, I'm sorry, I'm sorry I never told you how you take my breath away every time I see you. How a part of me dies every time I have to say goodbye. How the idea of living the rest of my life without you makes me feel sick.

I know I haven't got a lot to give Ellen, but everything I am... all of it... is yours. It was from the first time you stood there in front of me holding that cupcake.

(A now tearful Ellen is even more tearful)

ELLEN

I didn't make it...

MATT

What?

ELLEN

Matt I can't cook. I bought that from the shop. I wanted to impress you but the one I made looked awful.

(They both giggle)

MATT

Can I be the one that holds your hand and takes you on proper dates?

ELLEN

Yes.

(They Kiss. Jaz and Pete share a smile and then Hi five)

JAZ/PETE

Bosh.

(Ellen now understanding the board

smiles and then Kisses
Matt again)

THE END

David Proud

2016 marked David's decade anniversary working as a disabled Actor, Writer and Producer in the UK Film and TV industry. He is most well known for making history becoming the first regular disabled cast member of BBC prime time continuing drama EastEnders in 2010. He has also appeared in Secret Diary of a Call Girl, Best of Men, Siblings and No Offence and other leading roles. He has worked for leading broadcasters, the BBC, ITV and Channel 4. David has appeared in three independent UK feature films that have been seen worldwide in film festivals. As a producer, he has worked on short films, corporate videos, and up to feature film length. He has continued to develop projects featuring disability representation, as a disabled artist it is his passion. Other works include working as a freelance development producer for 104 Films from 2012 - 2016. As a writer, he is currently commissioned by BBC Films as a consultant on a feature film in development. In 2015 he was named in the Shaw Trust Power 100 as one of the most influential disabled people in the UK. In 2011 he was awarded the freedom of the city of London for his work with several charities. He is also a full voting member of BAFTA. In all of his work he is looking to bring authentic portrayals of disability to screen while retaining commercial value for investors.

With Thanks

I would like to thank the following people for helping to develop this script and for the table reads that helped shape it.

Rikki Beadle Blair, John Gordon, Jason Maza, Ashley Kumar, Samantha Lyden, Vanessa Carr, Vanessa Mayfield, Louisa Lytton, Rebecca Ferdinando and Jack Shalloo. You are all such talented beans and I look forward to our next artistic adventure.

I would also like to thank my parents for encouraging me to express myself without reservation or hesitation. My loving friends that gave me the inspiration behind this play. My son Isaac for brushing his teeth properly, going to bed on time, and for generally being the best son anyone could wish for. Last but no means least my beautiful wife for supporting me always in all ways. xxx

"The Art of Disability" – a handbook about disability representation in media, by David Proud, is available now at Amazon.

@prouddavid
@ambilobemedia
https://www.facebook.com/AmbilobeMedia
https://www.davidproud.co.uk

Lightning Source UK Ltd.
Milton Keynes UK
UKHW021242240422
401967UK00008B/261

9 781326 928100